FAIRY TALES GONE BAD

CREEPING BEAUTY

Joseph Coelho

Illustrated by

Freya Hartas

WALKER BOOKS

First published 2022 by Walker Books Ltd
87 Vauxhall Walk, London SE11 5HJ

2 4 6 8 10 9 7 5 3 1

Text © 2022 Joseph Coelho
Illustrations © 2022 Freya Hartas

The right of Joseph Coelho and Freya Hartas to be identified as author and
illustrator respectively of this work has been asserted in accordance with the
Copyright, Designs and Patents Act 1988

This book has been typeset in Archer

Printed and bound in China

British Library Cataloguing in Publication Data:
a catalogue record for this book is available from the British Library

ISBN 978-1-4063-8968-5

www.walker.co.uk

MIX
Paper | Supporting
responsible forestry
FSC® C144853
FSC
www.fsc.org

For the child reading this in a library ...
can you hear that bubbling sound?
That's the sound of new stories forming! – J.C.

In loving memory of Inky and Dracula,
who are now in catty heaven, sleeping and
creeping for all eternity. – F.H.

CONTENTS

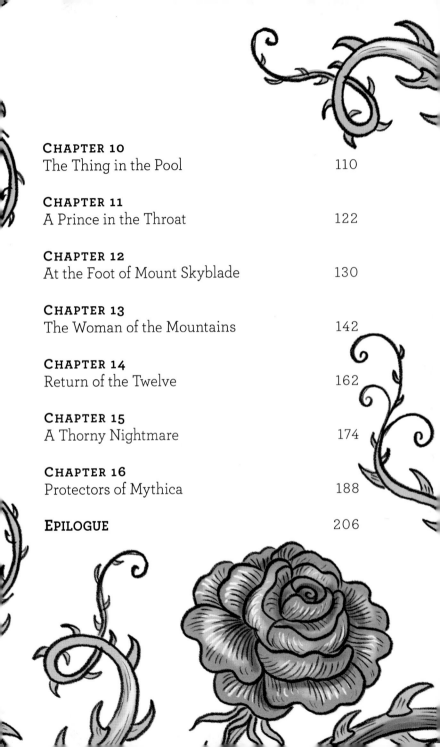

THE LIBRARY OF
FAIRY TALES GONE BAD

The Librarian

What's that noise?

Oh, it's you!
My lovely wretched readers.
Have you come to hear some
festering fables?
Some noxious narratives?
Well, you've come to the right place
for I am The Librarian
of Fairy Tales Gone Bad.

I discovered some neglected
tomes at the back of the library
some time ago.
They started off occupying
just one lonely shelf
of books left unread,
          unflicked through,
                    un-perused for so long
that the tales within them

had become
mouldy with changes,
sprouting new characters,
new twists and turns,
blooming with new beginnings
and middlings
and endings,
becoming something else,
becoming something ... BAD.

But since then,
my one lonely shelf
of frothing fairy tales
has grown,
has spread.
First it became a bookcase of
rancid retellings,
but now it has grown further,
bit by bit, stretching its tentacles,

taking over the entire library,
changing the very fabric of the building.

I have spent days
lost amongst the aisles
of The Library of Fairy Tales Gone Bad.
In the astronomy section
I discovered a horrid version
of *Hansel and Gretel* ...

Hansel and Gretel
and the Space-Witch!

In the biology section
I found a purulent version
of *Puss in Boots* ...
Octopus in Boots!

And in the fashion section
I found a whiffy version
of *The Elves and the Shoemaker* ...
The Elves and the Sweaty Trainer Remaker!

But in the botanical section
I found something altogether
shocking and frightening...
A story of fairy godmothers
and creeping vines,
of magical transformations,
and visions and signs!

This is the tale of ...

CREEPING BEAUTY.

CHAPTER 1

A Vision Lacking Precision

Eshe was one of thirteen sisters,
one of a set of tredecimalets!

Tre-deci-malets!!!

The youngest of a baker's dozen.
The sister who got to know her parents
for the least amount of time,
the one sister considered unlucky.

For even in Mythica,
thirteen is an unlucky number –
a number that is rarely spoken,
a number associated
with things that are broken.

But Eshe and her sisters
were special,

very special.

Known throughout
their tiny town of Fabledon
as gift-givers!
But not the kind of gifts
you could see with the eyes,

oh no!

The gifts they gave
were far greater than that.

Gifts of:

luck,

talent,

success,

imagination

and dreams!

That was, of course, if they liked you.
If they didn't,
those gifts
could just as easily become:

pestilence,

boils,

bad breath,

uncontrollable ear wax,

sneeze-laughing,

itching hiccups

and DEATH!!!

Yes, you heard that right ... DEATH!!!!!

So, everyone was kind to the sisters.
Everyone honoured them with the title of ...

Fairy Godmothers.

A title that had been bestowed
on all the women in their family
ever since the time before times.

They were invited to every party,
guests of honour at every christening
and followed on every social media platform.

So, none of them were surprised
when the invite arrived
for the christening of
Queen Araminta's daughter,
baby Princess Rose.

No one dared ask the queen
what had happened to Princess Rose's father,
the queen's one-time suitor.
It was a secret, and
so mighty was her rule,
and so terrible was her justice,
that no one dared ask.
But there were rumours...
Some believed she had eaten him!
Others, that he ran off as soon as he got a chance.
Rumours without end.

Eshe had odd stirrings
about the christening.
Her special ability
was different from that of her sisters.
Her ability was foresight.
Eshe could glimpse **THE FUTURE**.
But her ability came at a terrible price,
an unthinkable price,
a price more infuriating
than a head full of lice.
Eshe could only see
the most horrific of potential futures,
visions that would have her
screaming in the night,
scrabbling at her covers
and punching her pillow
(and sometimes even eating it!),
waking her sisters,
who'd comfort her
with worried looks.

However, none of Eshe's visions
had ever come to pass,
and so, even though her sisters adored her,
her abilities were doubted,
distrusted,
discredited
and disbelieved.

*"Do you think you could predict
one true thing, Eshe?"*

laughed sister number four named Forula,
who tied her curls with bows of every colour.

"Just one tiny little correct prediction,"
teased sister number eight named Eightina,
who had weighty rings on every finger.

What her sisters didn't know
was that none of Eshe's visions had come true
because Eshe herself had saved the world –
on many occasions, from utter ruination!

After her vision of lights in the skies
she chased away an alien army
with a thousand blinking eyes.

After her vision of a werewolf plague
she hunted down the werewolf queen
and laid her in an early grave.

After her vision of a merman attack
she found their underwater lair
and sent them floundering back.

Eshe was a hero,
albeit a silent one,
a hero who had prevented
the world's greatest calamities,
casualties and maladies
and it was her curse
that no one would ever know.

When the invites
to Princess Rose's christening arrived,
Eshe was struck by another vision –
not a usual vision
of drought or zombie apocalypse or
meteor strike.
This was far more terrifying...

In her vision she saw a world
blanketed in thorns!
Hungry, biting thorns
that grew without end,
over buildings and streets,
through windows and over furniture.
She saw hordes of people running
from the creeping barbed vines.
She saw armies from countless kingdoms
battling the vines
with swords, axes,
shears and weedkiller!

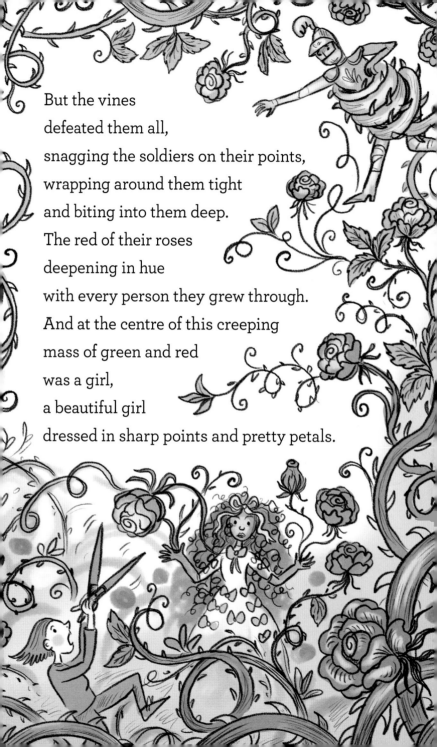

But the vines
defeated them all,
snagging the soldiers on their points,
wrapping around them tight
and biting into them deep.
The red of their roses
deepening in hue
with every person they grew through.
And at the centre of this creeping
mass of green and red
was a girl,
a beautiful girl
dressed in sharp points and pretty petals.

Eshe was on the floor
by the door
howling into her sister's
mountain of post.

"What is wrong?" cried her sisters.

"I had a vision."

"Oh no!" said sister number two
named Tutu (who was covered in tattoos).
*"Not another vision
lacking precision."*

"That's a good one, Tutu,"
said sister number one named Oneie,
who was never seen without her tiny
matchstick-box dog.

Eshe ignored their teasing
and instead told them
of vines that would creep
and bite
and cover the world,
and at their centre
a terrible queen
of things barbed and green
whom she called ...

Thorny Rose.

"She will look beautiful to all the world.
Her voice will be a melody of summer rain;
her laughter, the twinkling of the stars.
But she will change.
The very plants of the world will
do her bidding.
Her heart will harden and crack
and Thorny Rose will make the world
a bed for her barbs."

"And how will this happen?" asked her sisters.

"I don't know," said Eshe.

"And why will this happen?" asked her sisters.

"I don't know," said Eshe.

"And can you prove this will happen?" asked her sisters.

"I cannot," said Eshe.

And her sisters laughed
as they gathered up their invitations
(and fan mail)
and cuddly toys
(and Mevideo awards)
and boxes of chocolates
(and online-advert royalties)
and left poor Eshe alone
as they left to shop
for new christening outfits.

CHAPTER 2

A Question of Gifts

The days
leading up to the christening
were the hardest.

Eshe's thoughts were filled
with that horrid future.
But what could she do?
She could hardly
tell Queen Araminta
     that her daughter
          would slaughter
the world with thorns!

She had to act,
the world needed her
again!
She had to go to the christening.

There was one thing she could try ...
but it was risky.
It would require old magic,
deep and powerful magic.

And she would need to use her ...

Eye of Grimm!

A magical,

mystical,

alchemistical golden sphere!

Every magic wielder had one.
An object to help them
control their powers
and stop
some of the nastier side effects.

Eshe knew that she and her sisters
would be required to give gifts
to Queen Araminta's daughter.
Eshe, being differently endowed,
would normally give a reading
about the baby's good future fortune.
A fake reading, of course.
What good would it do
to tell people of the true horrors
Eshe so often saw?

It was not in Eshe's power
to bestow gifts
like her sisters did,

gifts that worked
and issued from their fingertips
in a cascade of magical sparkles.
But there were other ways
and other means to become temporarily
able to wield such magic.

It would not be expected,
but if she was able to bestow a gift
upon Queen Araminta's daughter
just like her sisters,
she could sneak in some spell
to change the princess's nature,
to stop her becoming
the evil queen
she had foreseen.
But to do this
she would need help.
She would need to meet with
the Woman of the Woods.

CHAPTER 3

The Woman of the Woods

The Woman of the Woods
was known to all the sisters,
but only Eshe visited her.

Eshe's sisters called her Witch
and Warlock and other foul names.
Their magic was all for show,
all for popularity and gaining favour,
magic that gave beauty and success,
popularity or a new dress!
They had no interest in the
old ways,

the ancient ways,
the magic-to-help-or-hinder ways.
The kind of magic that
the Woman of the Woods wielded,
ancient magic that was never gilded.

Magic that could make one
studious or resilient,
hard-working or secretly brilliant.

The Woman of the Woods
made a natural friend for Eshe.
Eshe so often needed tools from her,
tools that could defeat the calamities
that so often threatened the world. Tools like:

wands that fire fireballs,
curses created from entrails,
one-time spells to weaken and age
and occasionally maim!

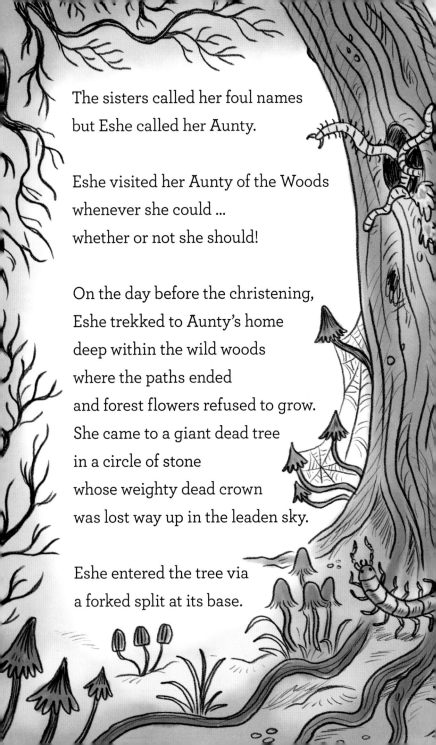

The sisters called her foul names
but Eshe called her Aunty.

Eshe visited her Aunty of the Woods
whenever she could ...
whether or not she should!

On the day before the christening,
Eshe trekked to Aunty's home
deep within the wild woods
where the paths ended
and forest flowers refused to grow.
She came to a giant dead tree
in a circle of stone
whose weighty dead crown
was lost way up in the leaden sky.

Eshe entered the tree via
a forked split at its base.

She loved the climb up to Aunty's.
She loved the smell of the wood
inside the trunk,
loved the way the surface
crumbled slightly under her fingers
as she climbed up,
passing crawling earwigs
and slithering snails,
skittering spiders
and things with stings in their tails.

Near the top of the trunk
was another opening
that opened up onto a plateau
of fused branches
littered with bones.

Aunty was nowhere to be seen
but her cauldron was there
frothing and sloshing,
bubbling and wobbling,
so Eshe decided to wait.

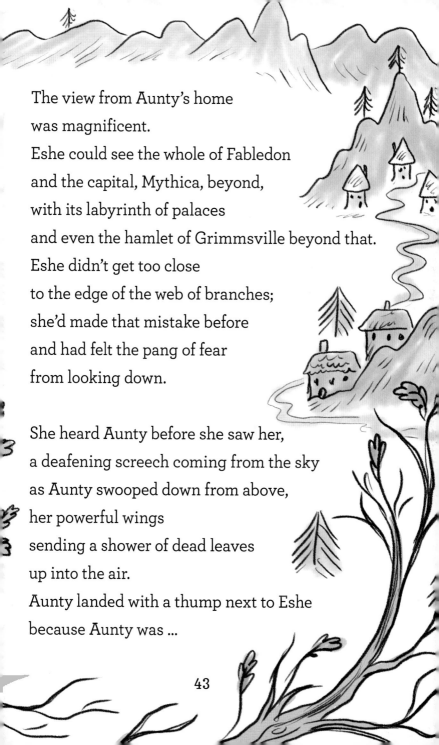

The view from Aunty's home
was magnificent.
Eshe could see the whole of Fabledon
and the capital, Mythica, beyond,
with its labyrinth of palaces
and even the hamlet of Grimmsville beyond that.
Eshe didn't get too close
to the edge of the web of branches;
she'd made that mistake before
and had felt the pang of fear
from looking down.

She heard Aunty before she saw her,
a deafening screech coming from the sky
as Aunty swooped down from above,
her powerful wings
sending a shower of dead leaves
up into the air.
Aunty landed with a thump next to Eshe
because Aunty was ...

a Harpy!

Both woman and bird,
both scowl and fowl,
with the body and head of a human,
but the wings and talons
of an almightily-powerful bird.

44

She hadn't always been this way.
This was the result of using magic
both ancient and dark,
     both growl and bark,
          both burn and spark.
The kind of magic
that puts hairs on your chest,
a beak on your mouth
and talons on your fingertips.

The kind of magic
that would let you fly
at the cost of rarely being able to land.
A magic that took as much as it gave,
if not more,
twisting the mind in the process
and settling something dark and solid
into the heart.

She landed next to Eshe with a bump,
her large, dark, owl-like eyes
gazing beyond Eshe
at the mountains in the distance.

"I love the view from here,"
said Eshe, following her gaze.

"It is amazing what you can see
from this height,
but I always want to get higher.
I know why you are here,"
cawed Aunty, as she eyed Eshe
with her piercing gaze.

"The cauldron reveals all.
You want to stop the future getting worse
with the aid of a little curse."

"No, Aunty! Not a curse!
I want to help the princess.
I want to stop her becoming ...

EVIL!"

Aunty flapped her wings in annoyance.

"Your heart is too kind, young Eshe.
Some people, some beings,
can only be evil,
have nothing in their hearts
but malice and cruelty.
I have also glimpsed the future
and this queen of thorns,
this princess,
will destroy everything."

Eshe threw her arms around Aunty.

"That's why I have you
to help me
    help her
        become something else,
            become something good."

Aunty softened
as she always did
whenever Eshe hugged.

"We can try,
young Eshe.
But what you ask
might be impossible,
uncrossable
and might involve the shockable!
Is it worth gambling
with the future of the world?"

"Yes, Aunty, it is.
If we don't try to save one,
we will never save all."

**"Very well,
young Eshe,
I will help stop
what you fear.
But first you must get me
some magical gear."**

"Like what?"
asked Eshe, noticing an unusual glint
in Aunty's eyes.

"Oh, not much. Just...

A pinch of snot
from a troll with a cold.
A toenail from a granny –
terribly old.

A slither of wart
from a dead man's hand.
A single note
from an old brass band.

The eye of a storm
and a patter of rain.
A lingering squelch
from a gurgling drain.

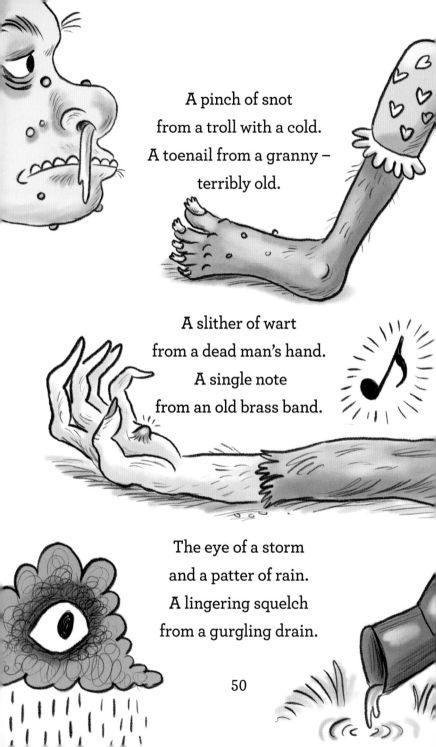

A thorn from a rose –
rotten at the core.
The bark from a dog
who doesn't bark any more.

And all this I need
before the moon shines tonight.
Get me all of these things,
and all will be right!"

"Thank you, Aunty," chimed Eshe,
as she disappeared down the trunk
and into the woods.
Eshe was no stranger
to the ingredients listed;
she knew exactly where to go...

CHAPTER 4

Weaving a Gift into a Curse

With the ingredients list
jingling in her head,
Eshe headed out...

To the old cassette store
for the deceased dog's bark.

A rotten-core-rose thorn
plucked from an old, abandoned park.

A lingering squelch
scooped from a hair-clogged drain.

She stole a storm's eye
and pocketed its rain.

A sad, dusty note
from a rusted robot band.

A shaving of wart
from a Mr Deadman's hand.

To the nail salon
to pedicure a gnarled toe.

And a final pinch
from a troll-nose with good flow!

All these things Eshe collected
before the sun set in the sky
and delivered to Aunty.

53

Aunty boiled the ingredients,
adding a tail feather of her own
and muttering in that language
of curses that very few know.

The resulting concoction
bubbled and stank.

54

She bottled it up and handed it to Eshe.

"Drop your Eye of Grimm in this tonight

and by tomorrow's christening

you will have power,

the same power as your sisters,

the power to gift or to curse,

to give life or an early hearse.

Remember all I have taught you

and choose your words well.

For the words of a curse

are important.

A sorceress must say what she means

or risk

not meaning what she says!"

Eshe took the bottle with thanks
and rushed home,
where her sisters were busy preparing
for tomorrow's christening.

"Where have you been, Eshe?"
said sister number nine named Jas-nine,
who had a beautiful pet llama with long,
luscious eyelashes.

"Nowhere," said Eshe, knowing that if her sisters
got the merest hint of what she planned to do,
they would stop her.

"I've just been getting ready for tomorrow,"
she lied, as she rushed off to her room before
her sisters could spot the nervous shuffling
she always did when lying.

In her room, Eshe plopped
her Eye of Grimm
into the fizzing concoction
and let it soak.
The Eye of Grimm
was like a part of herself,
her magical essence
made physical.
Every magical person had one.
They would appear
sometime around your eighth birthday,
floating by your bed
or popped in a shoe.
No one knew where they came from,
though she'd heard rumours
that your parents put them there.
You had to look after it.
Lose it, and you'd risk
being subject
to the chaotic nature of magic.

57

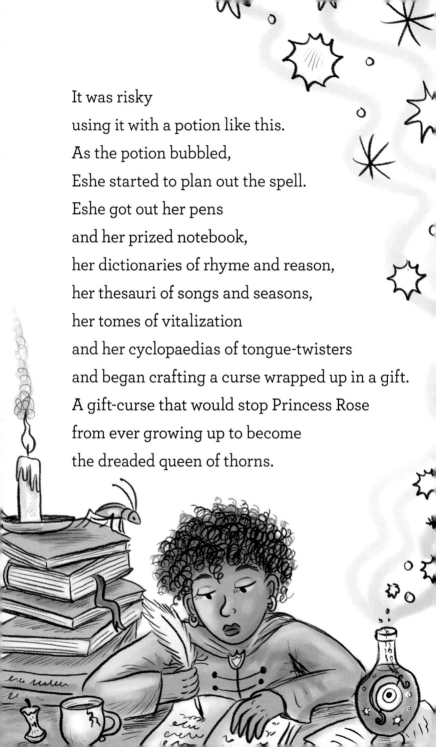

It was risky
using it with a potion like this.
As the potion bubbled,
Eshe started to plan out the spell.
Eshe got out her pens
and her prized notebook,
her dictionaries of rhyme and reason,
her thesauri of songs and seasons,
her tomes of vitalization
and her cyclopaedias of tongue-twisters
and began crafting a curse wrapped up in a gift.
A gift-curse that would stop Princess Rose
from ever growing up to become
the dreaded queen of thorns.

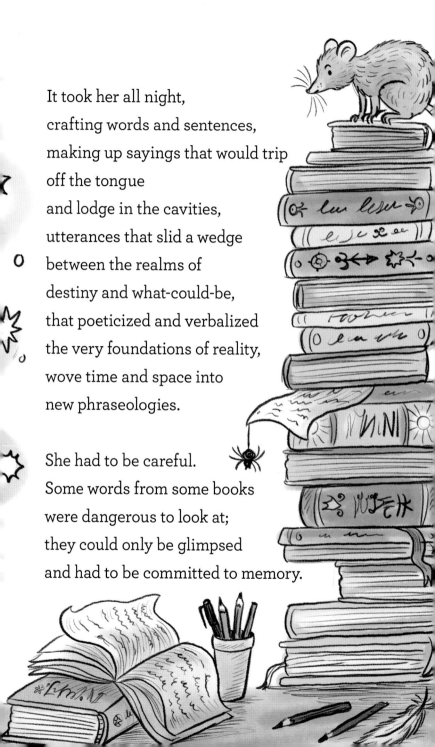

It took her all night,
crafting words and sentences,
making up sayings that would trip
off the tongue
and lodge in the cavities,
utterances that slid a wedge
between the realms of
destiny and what-could-be,
that poeticized and verbalized
the very foundations of reality,
wove time and space into
new phraseologies.

She had to be careful.
Some words from some books
were dangerous to look at;
they could only be glimpsed
and had to be committed to memory.

Other words needed to be written out
a hundred times over
before their true meaning could shine.
Using magic was hard work.
That's why her sisters
so often relied on a stock of a few learnt spells,
and certainly never made a spell up on the spot.
The sorceresses capable of freestyling a spell
were very few and far between.

By morning,
her gift-curse was ready and fitted neatly
on a small square of sable-leaf
which she memorized
and then swallowed.
For no curse, not even a gift-curse,
should ever be recorded.
She put on her fancy shoes
and joined her sisters
as they left for the christening.

CHAPTER 5

The Christening

The christening
was a small and cheap affair,
the smallest to have ever been held
in Fabledon
in living memory.
But then Queen Araminta
was not one for celebration or fancy.
She was seen as a cruel and hard ruler.

Those who remembered her mother,
Queen Mintaram,
fought back tears,

thinking on how prosperous
Fabledon had once been,
how no one had wanted for anything,
how help and support had been given
to all who needed them.
Since Queen Araminta had come to power,
support had been cut;
everyone was expected to make do
and to do well.
And if they could not,
well, whose fault was it but their own?
As a result,
the whole of Fabledon suffered.
The sick and needy wandered the streets,
shops went out of business
and those that could
left for the other cities and towns of Mythica
where outsiders were welcomed
and skills valued.

Eshe and her sisters
approached Queen Araminta's
wooden palace with their hearts
thumping in their chests.
The whole palace was wooden.
Everything inside was wood, too:
every door, every item of furniture,
every lamp and fixture.
The lampshades – sheets of wood, paper-thin.
The pillows on the chairs – wood.
Rumour had it that Queen Araminta even slept
under wafer-thin sheets of bark.
But this palace had not been built this way.
Many remembered a time
when it was stone and brick,
when the cushions were soft
and the curtains flowing.
There was magic in the walls.
A spell of old, dark magic.

There were no crowds to navigate,
no banners celebrating the new
baby princess –
just a line of guards,
wooden guards,
that stared with unchanging wooden faces.

The guards creaked as they lowered
their splintered shields
and woodwormed swords
to let the sisters pass
into the inner courtyard.

There sat Queen Araminta.
Her tall crown of dead branches
made her look terrifying
as she gazed down at them
with her amber-coloured eyes.
She was wrapped tightly
in a tree-moss dress of grey and green.

Princess Rose was in a rocking crib
being mechanically rocked
by a wooden guard.

"You have come to give your gifts,
godmothers?"
asked the queen, with a voice
like dry leaves.

"Yes, Your Majesty," stammered Oneie,
as her tiny matchstick-box dog
yelped and closed its match-box tight.

"You may approach the princess
and bestow your gifts,"
crinkled the queen.

The sisters approached,
stretching their arms up high to the sky,
preparing for their gift-giving routine,
a well-known spectacle
that at past christenings
would have been viewed by hundreds,
thousands –
thundreds! – of people.
But today,
only the queen looked on
with her host of deadwood guards.

Being the oldest, Oneie began
and the rest followed suit...

*"I'm the first of the sisters
and I give to thee
a smile of sunshine that beams beautifully."*

*"I'm the second of the sisters
and to you I bestow
eyes that shine with their own super glow."*

*"I'm the third of the sisters
and from my sparkling hand
I give you a dress sense that is wonderfully
grand."*

"I'm the fourth of the sisters.
What gift shall I entrust?
Incredible hair with a hint of gold dust."

Eshe was getting nervous.
Would the queen notice the curse
within her gift?
And if she did, would Eshe ever escape
the creaking palace
and its splintered soldiers?

"I'm the fifth of the sisters
and to you I confer
a sweet perfume of spices and myrrh."

"I'm the sixth of the sisters
and I'll parcel out
a wondrous beauty that no one dare doubt."

"I'm the seventh of the sisters
and to you I transmit
a smidgen of amusing –
never embarrassing – wit."

"I'm the eighth of the sisters
and to you I deliver
a beautiful laugh that sounds like a river."

Eshe's turn was fast approaching.
She couldn't help but notice
how shallow her sisters' gifts were.
But at least none of them had a sting in their
tail like hers...

*"I'm the ninth of the sisters
and to you I hand over
an online following that will forever spill over."*

*"I'm the tenth of the sisters
and to you I consign
that your every makeover will be of impeccable
design."*

Eshe's heart became a drum roll.
This was it, two more gifts
and then it would be her turn.
She started to fret... Had she memorized the
gift-curse correctly?
What if something went wrong?!
A slip of a single word
could consign the poor child to death!

"I'm the eleventh of the sisters
and to you I award
that no matter how dull the company,
you'll never grow bored."

"I'm the twelfth of the sisters
and to you I donate
a store of gold coins of incredible weight."

It was Eshe's turn.
She approached,
sweat pooling in her hands,
her heart all a-flutter.
She gazed down into the crib
and little baby Princess Rose gazed up,
all smiles and gurgles,
all baby joy and delight.

I can't gift-curse this child;
she hasn't done anything wrong yet,
she thought.

But then the memory of her vision came crashing in,
a world consumed by thorns,
where darkness ruled
and none were safe and so...
She parted her lips
to gift-curse the child,
when from above came a ...

SCCCCCRRRREEEEEEEECCCCHHHHHHHHHH!

And down from the sky
tumbled –
in a mass of feathers and talons –

AUNTY!

CHAPTER 6

Freestyling a Spell

She circled mere metres above the child,
wings spread like a terrible plague.
The queen's guards creaked into action,
readying their splinter spears
and nocking their thorn arrows.
But it was useless. No weapon even got close
as Aunty began to mumble and curse.
A web of pulsating purple and green
mists encircled Aunty and child alike,
as Aunty's curse rained down...

"No gift from me,
no boon, no bounty.
My words will comfort no more.
For when this girl
reaches sixteen,
she'll drop down dead
to the floor.
Dead as a dodo,
dead as a dog,
dead as a single missed beat."

"No, Aunty!" cried Eshe. "You mustn't."
For it was clear what she intended.
Aunty was taking matters into her own hands and
was intent on cursing the child
with an early grave.

"Leave me, Eshe.
You haven't the nerve
to do what must be done.
You have seen the future;
you have seen what she will become."

And, with that, Aunty continued her curse...

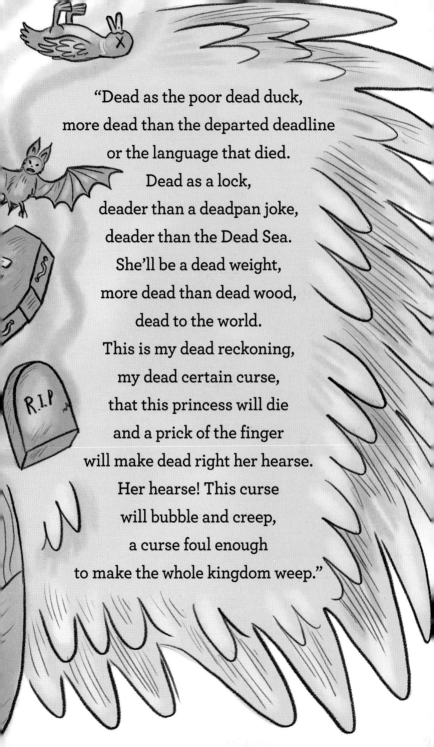

"Dead as the poor dead duck,
more dead than the departed deadline
or the language that died.
Dead as a lock,
deader than a deadpan joke,
deader than the Dead Sea.
She'll be a dead weight,
more dead than dead wood,
dead to the world.
This is my dead reckoning,
my dead certain curse,
that this princess will die
and a prick of the finger
will make dead right her hearse.
Her hearse! This curse
will bubble and creep,
a curse foul enough
to make the whole kingdom weep."

The ball of glowing energy
that surrounded the harpy and the child
exploded, leaving a whispering on the wind
of ...

"WEEP ...

wEEP ...

weEP ...

weeP ...

weep

eep

ep

p."

Queen Araminta stood and screamed
as Aunty flapped up and away,
her curse in place.
Eshe ran to the crib.

"What are you doing?!" cried the queen.
"Your kind have done enough damage here."

The queen's woody guards
surrounded the princess's crib.

"I can help, Your Majesty.
Let me lessen this curse –
I am yet to give my gift."

The queen nodded,
the guards creaked back,
and Eshe thought quickly,
whilst the magic of the curse
still lingered in the air.
She had to do the impossible
and freestyle this curse into a gift.
And to trick the magic into thinking
the spell wasn't over,

she'd have to use the last word of the spell
to create something new...

"Weep! Weep!
The whole kingdom will weep,
but their tears won't fall long
for the princess is just asleep!
Asleep, asleep,
no death at her door..."

Eshe struggled to remember
the words used in the curse,
words that would have to be
reused and reshaped.
Just one kept leaping into her mind.
She had to act,
for the magic was fading,
the curse was setting...

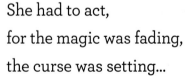
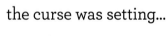

"Not dead,
not dead, not dead.
Not at all like dead wood,
but living and growing
like a successful ruler should.
A prick to the finger
will not spell out doom.
But instead, a sleep
that will blossom and bloom."

The spell was mangled and rough
but Eshe hoped she had reduced the damage,
changed the curse from a death to a sleep,
from dying to dreaming.

CHAPTER 7

Thorny Rose

Princess Rose
was a lovely child.
At fifteen years old,
all who met her agreed
that she had all the gifts
that the godmothers had bestowed upon her
and more.
She was kind,
she was polite
and she was smart.

Devilishly smart.

So smart that it took all
of Queen Araminta's energy
to keep her safe,

safe from her own
dangerous curiosity.
The curse,
spoken by Aunty the harpy
and softened by Eshe,
spoke of a prick to the finger.
And so Queen Araminta ensured
that all sharp objects
were removed from the kingdom.
So:

     no spindles,
   no needles,
     no pins,
   no badges,
     no hedgehogs,
   no porcupines,
     no barbecue skewers!
No sharpened pencils,
    no cocktail sticks
and no safety pins!

But young Princess Rose
always managed to find something sharp...

She would pluck splinters
from her mother's wooden guards
and prise nails out of floorboards,

find old badges in forgotten cupboards,

and discover cacti
in ancient parts of the garden.

And so her mother wrapped her
in cotton,
sewed her into her clothes,
put thick rubber gloves on her hands
and steel-toed boots on her feet,
all to protect her
from ever being pricked.

Princess Rose
grew up having never known
a bump
or a scratch,
a bruise or a cut.
She had been allowed no
pets with their risky claws,
was forbidden to climb trees
or run barefoot in long grass.
She never visited a beach
or played with a single toy
that harboured a corner or a hard edge.

Her world had been soft and safe
and oh-so boring.
The only person
whose life remained shrouded
in mystery and therefore
tinged with excitement
was Queen Araminta herself,
who would regularly retreat into the depths
of the dark forest
for days at a time.
No one knew where she went
and no one knew
what she did whilst she was there.

It was on one of these
sojourns in the dark forest
that everything changed.

Princess Rose, who was normally so good,
crept away from her guards of wood

to the central courtyard gardens
where a single rose stood.

    A rose missed by the gardeners,
    a rose that seemed to bloom under her gaze,
    a rose that seemed to sing to her,

its colours saturating
its smell giddying,
in a most unnatural –
most certainly magical – way!

Princess Rose's fingers ached to touch it,
yearned to feel it,
longed to reach out and hold it, and so ...
she removed one thick, rubber glove
from one dainty, never-calloused hand ...

and reached out to pluck the flower.

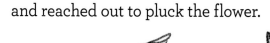

CHAPTER 8

A Nightmare-Filled Sleep

A life wrapped and swaddled
had taught Princess Rose nothing
of the thorns that roses conceal.
And it was on this,
her sixteenth birthday,
that Princess Rose
experienced, for the first time,
the insult that a flower can give
as her finger was pricked
and a single drop of blood
started to bloom.

The change started slowly at first...
Princess Rose fell into a slumber,
a deep sleep.
A deep, dream-filled sleep?
Nay! A deep, nightmare-filled sleep
that had her tossing and turning,
groaning and moaning.
And as she slept and dreamt,
the skin of her legs started to thicken
and crack like bark.
Her toes started to grow,
as did her legs
and fingers and arms,
all becoming vines,
vines covered with barbs,
from which deep-red roses
bloomed,
until the whole courtyard was filled
with flowers and thorns
that grew and crept.

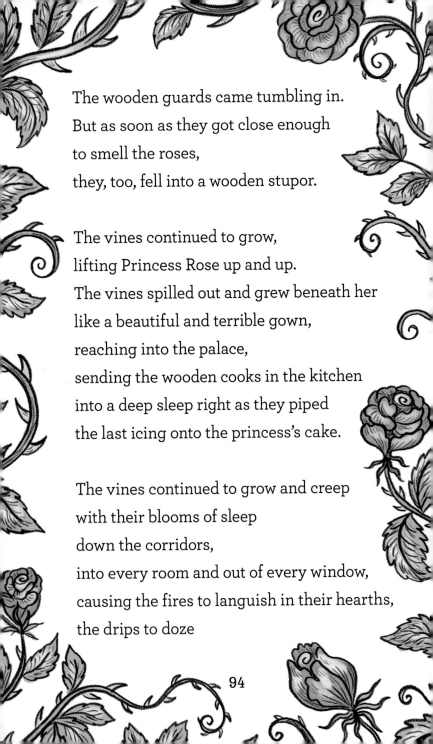

The wooden guards came tumbling in.
But as soon as they got close enough
to smell the roses,
they, too, fell into a wooden stupor.

The vines continued to grow,
lifting Princess Rose up and up.
The vines spilled out and grew beneath her
like a beautiful and terrible gown,
reaching into the palace,
sending the wooden cooks in the kitchen
into a deep sleep right as they piped
the last icing onto the princess's cake.

The vines continued to grow and creep
with their blooms of sleep
down the corridors,
into every room and out of every window,
causing the fires to languish in their hearths,
the drips to doze

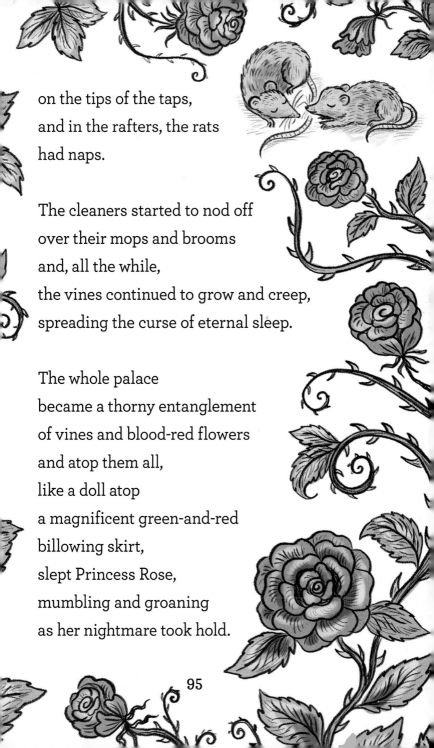

on the tips of the taps,
and in the rafters, the rats
had naps.

The cleaners started to nod off
over their mops and brooms
and, all the while,
the vines continued to grow and creep,
spreading the curse of eternal sleep.

The whole palace
became a thorny entanglement
of vines and blood-red flowers
and atop them all,
like a doll atop
a magnificent green-and-red
billowing skirt,
slept Princess Rose,
mumbling and groaning
as her nightmare took hold.

CHAPTER 9

Into the Woods

Ever since the curse,
the fairy godmothers had been
told (in no uncertain terms)
to stay away.
TO SKIP,
SCRAM,
FLEE!

"Don't you dare show your faces in my
kingdom again,"
creaked the queen.

The godmothers had not been invited
to any more christenings.
Their follower numbers shrank;
their Mevideo subscribers dwindled.
They became ... ordinary
and oh-so boring.

They blamed Eshe, of course.

"It's all your fault, unlucky Eshe,"
said sister number seven,
(called Sevoona, who always
wore magnificent hats).
*"You should know better
than to share our business with a harpy."*

Eshe neglected to mention
her original plan
to curse Princess Rose
and stop her vision coming true.

Taking all the blame
for the harpy's actions
became unpleasant,
and so Eshe left her home
and retreated deep into the dark forest
to live alone.

Once again, her actions to save the future
would go unrecognized,
　　　　overlooked,
　　　　　　　　unfamed and unhonoured.
Even if this time things
hadn't gone exactly to plan,
at least Princess Rose would sleep
and no longer be a threat.

Eshe never saw Aunty again.
Her coop high up in the tree
remained empty,
leaving Eshe totally alone.

Over the years,
Eshe committed herself
to magic and continuing her work,
stopping her terrifying visions
from coming true.

She had turned a horde of war-hungry trolls
into a harmless flock of hungry gulls.

She had reduced a world-blasting meteoroid
into a firework display that all enjoyed.

She convinced a town-guzzling dinosaur
to go elsewhere to try out his roar!

Over time,
she improved her abilities
beyond just foresight.
Now she could wield magic
without having to soak
her Eye of Grimm in potions.

But, as always, her heroics
went unnoticed,
undocumented,
devoid of praise
and bereft of appreciation.

So, it was a total surprise
when who should come knocking at her door
asking for help
but ...

Queen Araminta herself.

"You must help me!"
wailed the queen.

Eshe was suspicious.
She eyed the surrounding forest,
expecting a wooden guard
to come crashing through the tree line
with wooden sword raised.
When no attack came,
Eshe invited the queen inside.

The queen looked much older,
wrinkles had set in like cracks.
The terrifying regent
had been replaced by a mother
who looked scared, sad and alone.

"It's my daughter.
The curse has taken her."

"Oh, no! Has she died?"
cried out Eshe, fearful that her attempt
to weaken the spell had all been for nothing.

"No, not death,
and for that I am most grateful to you.
I laid so much blame at your door
but I shall do that no more.

You stopped a
far more terrible fate.
But whilst she has not died,
she has fallen asleep.
And as she sleeps ...
she creeps!

Thick, thorny vines
have erupted from her
and they grow and creep.
And wherever they grow,
all the people sleep."

Eshe rushed out of her home,
snatching a telescope from her shelves.

She climbed the nearest tree
and peered out in the direction of the palace.

Eshe was struck dumb.
There was Princess Rose
atop a mountain of thorns,
just like her vision had predicted.
How could this be?
Her actions had always prevented disaster,
never been the cause of it.
Sure, her softening of the curse
had been rushed,

but it couldn't have caused this!
Could it?

She leapt from the tree
and landed next to the queen.

"Your Majesty,
I get the feeling that
there is more to this story
and more to your daughter
than meets the eye."

Eshe noticed a twitch
in Queen Araminta's mouth,
a slight suggestion
of the younger, fiercer queen
that she had known
all those years ago.
But sadness quickly replaced
any ferocity.

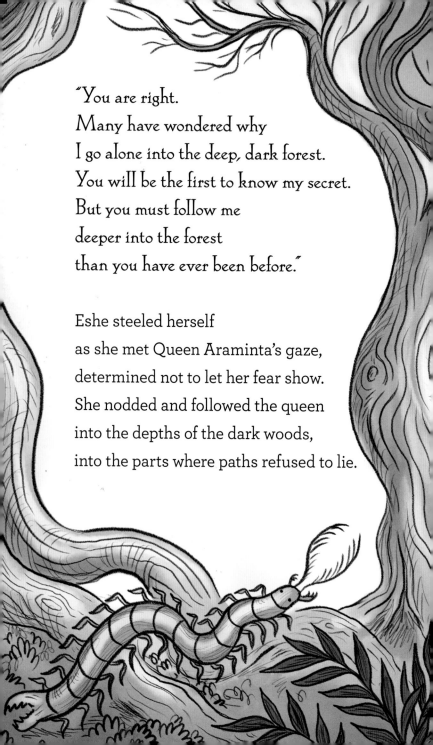

"You are right.
Many have wondered why
I go alone into the deep, dark forest.
You will be the first to know my secret.
But you must follow me
deeper into the forest
than you have ever been before."

Eshe steeled herself
as she met Queen Araminta's gaze,
determined not to let her fear show.
She nodded and followed the queen
into the depths of the dark woods,
into the parts where paths refused to lie.

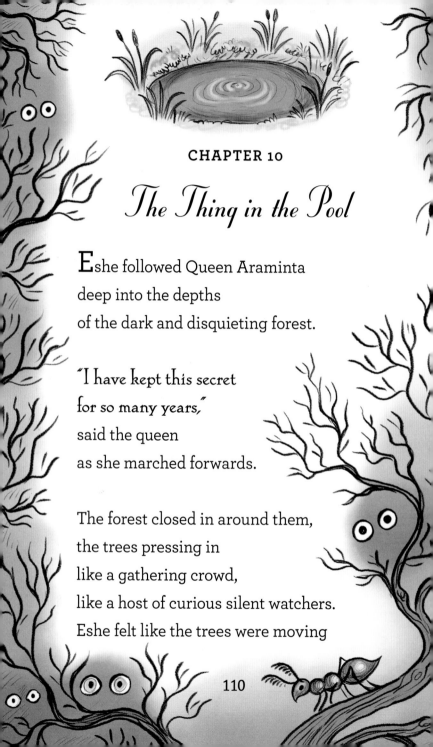

CHAPTER 10

The Thing in the Pool

Eshe followed Queen Araminta
deep into the depths
of the dark and disquieting forest.

"I have kept this secret
for so many years,"
said the queen
as she marched forwards.

The forest closed in around them,
the trees pressing in
like a gathering crowd,
like a host of curious silent watchers.
Eshe felt like the trees were moving

110

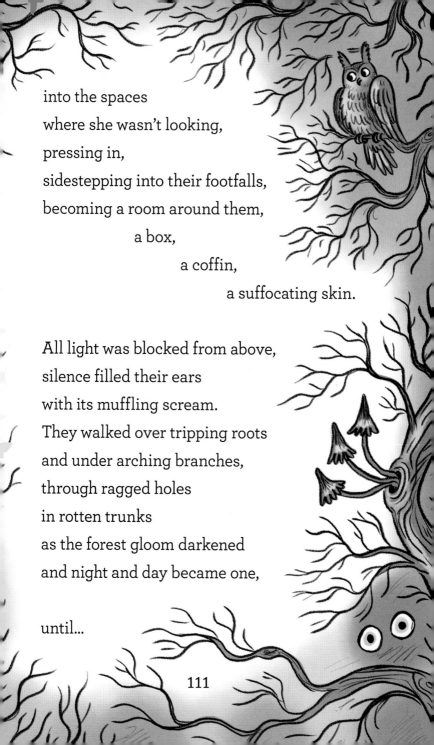

into the spaces
where she wasn't looking,
pressing in,
sidestepping into their footfalls,
becoming a room around them,
        a box,
               a coffin,
                   a suffocating skin.

All light was blocked from above,
silence filled their ears
with its muffling scream.
They walked over tripping roots
and under arching branches,
through ragged holes
in rotten trunks
as the forest gloom darkened
and night and day became one,

until...

They came to a clearing,
a breath amongst the trees.
And, at its centre ...

                lay a pool.
A perfectly round pool
with water deep,

            dark and distasteful.

By its edge
was a stump
with a top worn smooth.
Queen Araminta
sat upon it,
as she had done
so many times before,
and began her story.

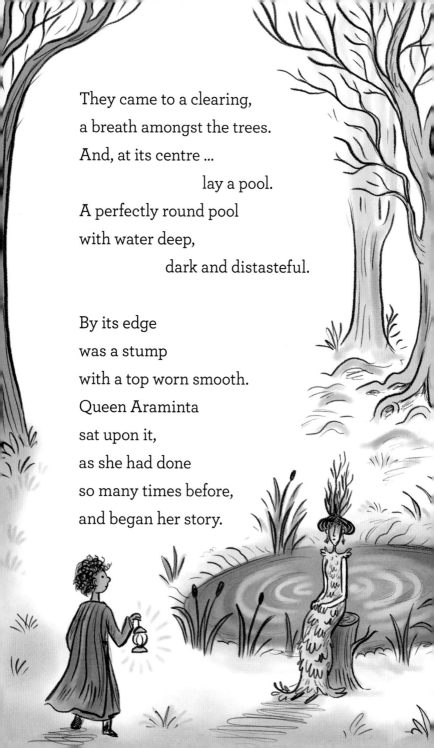

"I've always walked these woods
ever since my girlhood,
always gone deeper than I should
even when my parents told me not to.

My parents married me young
to a rich prince from a prosperous kingdom
on the other side of these woods.
I hated him until I learnt
that he liked to walk these woods, too.
And so we would walk these woods together
and a love between us grew.
But I never knew
that his path had been crossed by another.

A Woman of the Woods,
a caster of spells,
both ancient and dark."

Eshe gasped.

A Woman of the Woods!
Could the queen really be talking
about Aunty?
Maybe her sisters had been right
to be afraid for her all these years.

"My prince told me all about her,
how she was obsessed with him,
threatening him,
wanting him all to herself.

I would see her sometimes
skulking in the shadows,
following us as we walked.
She was a sad-looking woman then,
but also angry.
When I proposed to him,
she went mad.
The Woman of the Woods
took her revenge on us.

She spent the months of our honeymoon
learning the foulest magic
until it changed her,
made feathers sprout from her skin,
put a beak on her mouth.
When we came home, we found that she
had turned our palace and everything
and everyone in it into wood.

I see now that she was just testing her magic,
waiting to destroy my family entirely.

My husband marched alone
into the woods
to confront her,
to make her stop.
He found her here
in this place
and it was here that she changed him
for ever..."

115

From the pool came a bubbling.
Eshe edged closer
to peer down into its depths.
Something was rising up
through the water,
something with big, bulging eyes
and a huge, wide mouth.
Eshe fell backwards
as the largest frog
she had ever seen
emerged at the centre of the pool.
Its skin,
thick and warty;
its eyes, like two fiery spheres.
It sat in the middle of the pool,
its strange-shaped pupils
staring.

"What is that?"
asked Eshe, backing away.

"That was Princess Rose's father.
My prince, my love,
my husband,
before the Woman of the Woods
cast her spell, turning him into this,
and making the world forget
he ever existed."

"So, your family has been twice cursed.
Magic has already touched you all,"
said Eshe, as she realized why her actions
had not stopped her vision coming true
but had, in fact, fulfilled it.
Magic is a volatile thing and a little too much
can only result in chaos.

Queen Araminta approached the pool,
her hand stretched out before her.

"Is he safe?"
asked Eshe, as she watched the gigantic
frog's air sac quiver as the queen approached.

"I have come here to see him,
letting him get used to me.
Each time, I move a little nearer,
convinced that if he accepts me
and remembers our love,
then perhaps the curse will break."

The queen edged closer still
as a grumble started to rumble
deep within the giant frog's stomach.

"Your Majesty, this is old, deep magic.
I'm not sure that it can be lifted so easily,"
said Eshe, stepping back
away from the pool and the giant frog
as its grumbles became bellows.

"Look, he's letting me come closer.
This is the closest I've ever been.
Maybe it's because you're here.
Or maybe he senses
that something is wrong with our daughter."

Just at that moment,
a knight,
a knight on a mission,
a knight on a mission to save maidens,
came crashing through the trees
in shining armour of gold and silver
encrusted with jewels,
with a sword of twisted fire iron
and a helmet shaped like a barking stag.

"Never fear, ladies,
it is I, Sir Doo-Good.
I have come to the rescue.
I have heard of the sleeping beauty
atop the mountain of thorns
and I have come to save her
as only a knight can...
I have studied the thorns
and made enquiries into the barbs
and asked the world's finest experts
on the best ways to deal with such
a botanical calamity
and you need fear no longer for I am prepared.
I have read all the books,
I have extra-thick gardening gloves
and the best garden shears money can buy.
I shall defeat the vines,
or my name isn't Sir Doo-Good."

The giant frog
opened its gigantic mouth
and let rip a humongous slime-sparkling tongue
that whipped out lightning fast,
grabbed Sir Doo-Good around the waist ...

and swallowed him whole
before Sir Doo-Good had time
to consult his books,
don his gloves
or take out his garden shears.

CHAPTER 11

A Prince in the Throat

The giant frog
that had once been
Queen Araminta's prince
had swallowed a knight whole,
in one gulp,
without so much as a bite
or a chew
or a thank you!

Queen Araminta and Eshe
were shocked,
    dumbfounded,
            astounded!
The frog stared at them
with those fiery amber eyes
and started to open his mouth wide.

Without hesitation, Eshe threw up her hands
and started to freestyle a spell.

"You are a frog,
all hop and dive,
but far more than beast exists inside.
In truth, you are quite royal.

Free your mind
from this froggy form,
shake off this skin and transform,
and help ease your family's toil.

The surrounding trees
started to glow.
The air fell still,
but the trees continued to brighten.
The glow started to thrum,
low at first
and then louder,
until there was a ...

      thunder-striking-boom-
            banging-eardrum-aching clap!

The giant frog
was still in the pool,
unchanged,
save for his eyes.
His eyes no longer held the same menace,
no longer scanned them
with a lava indifference.

He opened his mouth and began to croak.

The croak became a gurgled choke,
from which words
started to emerge...

"My love,
I am back,"
croaked the frog,
as his globular eyes
swivelled onto the queen.

"Paulsgrave? My prince?
Is that you?
Have you returned to me?"

The frog looked at his reflection
in the still waters of the pool.

"But perhaps only in mind."

Eshe relaxed her spell-casting stance.

"The magic was deep within you,
Your Highness.
It will take a greater power than mine
to return you to your full form."

Another rumble
came vibrating through the woods.
Eshe wondered if it was another knight
who'd heard the tale of the sleeping beauty
come to save the day
and noticed how Prince Paulsgrave's
froggy tongue
licked his toady lips
in froggy anticipation
of another quick meal.

But no saviour
came crashing through the trees.

Instead, what came a-creeping
were vines,
thick, thorny vines,
waves of them
tearing down and covering the trees
in their prickly spitefulness.
And way off
in the distance,
atop the advancing
mountain of barbs,
wobbled the Creeping Beauty
Princess Rose
in a flower-scented nightmare.

"We have to flee,"
        shouted Eshe.

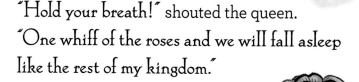

"Hold your breath!" shouted the queen.
"One whiff of the roses and we will fall asleep
like the rest of my kingdom."

127

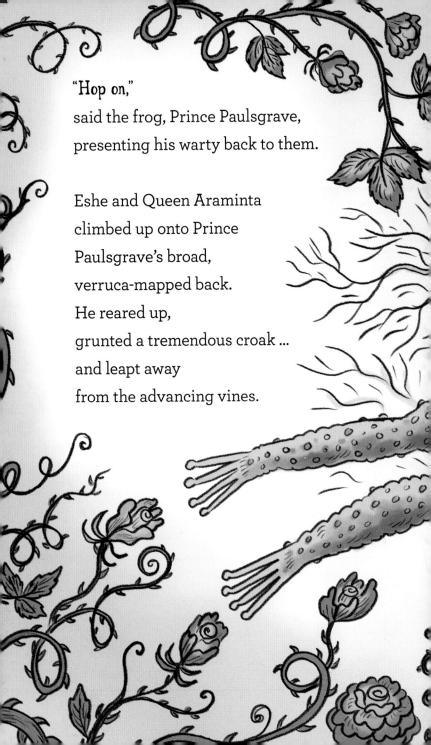

"Hop on,"
said the frog, Prince Paulsgrave,
presenting his warty back to them.

Eshe and Queen Araminta
climbed up onto Prince
Paulsgrave's broad,
verruca-mapped back.
He reared up,
grunted a tremendous croak ...
and leapt away
from the advancing vines.

CHAPTER 12

At the Foot of Mount Skyblade

They leapt
   and bounced,
      and bounded and hopped,
   rocketed and soared
through the winding trees of the dark forest.
The frog prince
using his large feet
to climb up one tree and then leap
to another,
the webbing between his large toes
acting as parachutes as he sailed
between the trunks,

z z

grabbing hold
and launching off again.

The vines of Creeping Beauty followed,
the sickly-sweet scent of her flowers
making all that smelled them
sleep, doze,
slumber and snooze.

The three watched
as rivers dozed on their beds
and birds napped on the wing,
and all the time
a deep snoring
followed them,
getting louder and louder
as more joined
the eternal sleep.

"What are those vines?"
asked the frog prince in a croak.

"Those vines are your daughter.
She was cursed to die
by the Woman of the Woods.
Eshe here softened the curse to a sleep,
but something has gone wrong
and now she grows and creeps."

The frog prince
made a strange gurgling sound
at the back of his throat.

"Oh, my prince,
it's not your fault.
She has been after
our family for years,"
said the queen, gritting her teeth.
"But we will put an end to it
once and for all."

The frog prince leapt further and further,
going faster and faster,
until the creeping vines were far behind them.
They stopped to rest
by the ruin of an old mill.

Eshe took out her Eye of Grimm
and prepared a food spell.

"What is that?"
asked the queen.

"It's my Eye of Grimm,
my magical essence.
Every sorceress has one.
It helps us focus our magic
and stops any unfortunate side effects
from the harder spells.

My sister Jas-nine once lost hers
and every time she cast a spell,
one of her fingers would turn into a toe.
She ended up with very smelly hands.
Luckily, we found it down the back of the sofa
and she got all her fingers back,"

said Eshe, and a sadness bloomed in her
as she thought about her sisters
and the years it had been since
she had seen them.

"Fascinating,"
said the queen.
"Look at this, Paulsgrave. Eshe is
going to cast a spell."

From a distance, Paulsgrave stared,
his eyes wide and scared.

Eshe focused her mind
and began her spell...

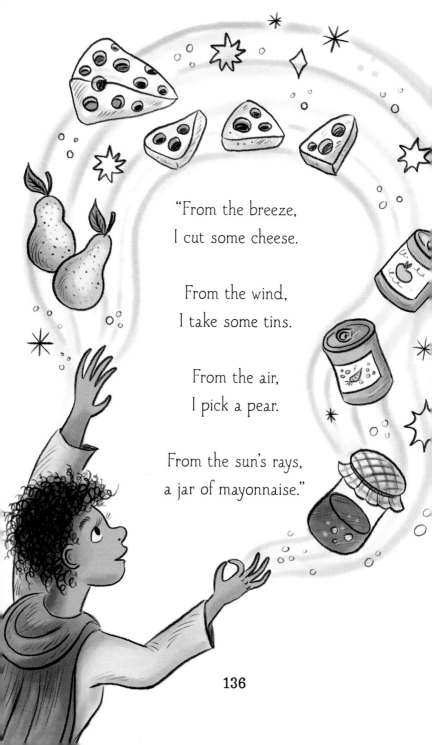

"From the breeze,
I cut some cheese.

From the wind,
I take some tins.

From the air,
I pick a pear.

From the sun's rays,
a jar of mayonnaise."

136

Food swirled out of the air,
a strange concoction
of airy Swiss cheese
and flying fish fillets,
blush pears
and spicy, hot mayonnaise.

As they sat and chewed
and gulped
their free food,
they heard the sound of feet,
marching,

      stamping,

           tramping

                feet,

as over the hills came ...

an army.

It was an enormous army
carrying the banners of one of the
neighbouring kingdoms,
led by a fiery warrior knight.

"What are you doing?"
asked Eshe,
as the fiery warrior knight
rode up to them,
wearing her armour of lava stone.

138

"I am the Warrior Knight
and I have heard of a danger up ahead
and I shall defeat it."

"What have you heard about the danger?"
asked Eshe.

"I don't listen to stories or hearsay – I rush ahead.
That's the only way to deal with a danger,
straight in and let it meet
your pointy stick and be done with.
That's enough chit-chat for now.
My army and I have a danger to conquer.
No doubt it's just beyond those vines
in the distance there."

And with that, the Warrior Knight
reared up on her steed and raced off
towards the advancing vines,
her army following dutifully behind.

139

Eshe watched with her telescope
as the Warrior Knight
ran head first into the brambles
only to nod off immediately
and disappear beneath
the undergrowth,
never to be seen again.

"Seems like the whole of Mythica
has gone mad. We need to stop the curse
and I think I know how.
I have to speak to the Woman of the Woods.
She knows me.
I can convince her to stop this madness,
I'm sure I can."

"Will she listen to you?
Do you even know where she is?"
asked the queen.

"I have to try; it's our only hope
and I have an idea of where she might be."

Eshe pointed
at the snowy cap
of Mount Skyblade
that lay on the horizon,
angling her index finger
up to the highest peak.

"If she's anywhere,
she'll be there."

CHAPTER 13

The Woman of the Mountains

The climb to the mountain's peak
was hard.
It was too cold and slippery for Paulsgrave
to carry them,
so they trekked
slowly up its mountainous paths,
hugging their clothes tight around them
as the temperature dropped
and the snow flurries stung their eyes.

At the summit,
the three came to a howling cave,
a deep purple light
pulsating within it.

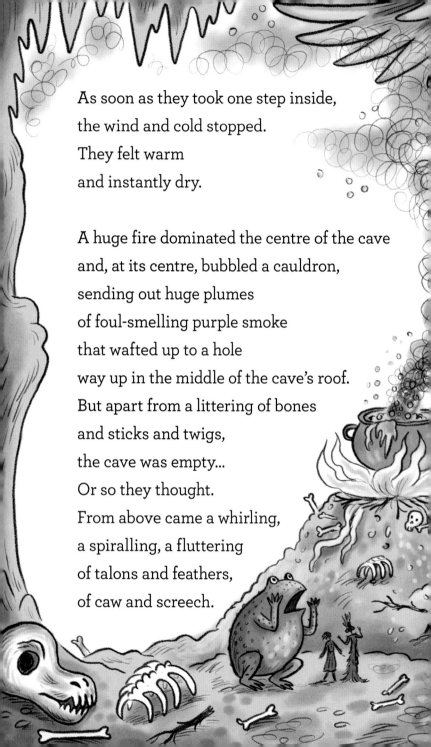

As soon as they took one step inside,
the wind and cold stopped.
They felt warm
and instantly dry.

A huge fire dominated the centre of the cave
and, at its centre, bubbled a cauldron,
sending out huge plumes
of foul-smelling purple smoke
that wafted up to a hole
way up in the middle of the cave's roof.
But apart from a littering of bones
and sticks and twigs,
the cave was empty...
Or so they thought.
From above came a whirling,
a spiralling, a fluttering
of talons and feathers,
of caw and screech.

Eshe was first to realize
that it was Aunty,
the Woman of the Woods.
But in the years that had passed
since she had last seen her,
she had changed.
She had become
more bird-like,
more monstrous.
Gone was the playful glint in the eye –
it had been replaced by something
far nastier.
And she was huge,
much bigger than before,
more like a dragon than a bird,
a bird-like dragon.

145

She circled around them,
cawing loud enough
to hurt the ears
and make the bones ring.

"Aunty! It is me, Eshe...
We need you to reverse
your curse."

But Aunty wasn't listening;
she was circling,
circling and screeching,
her clutching talons
getting dangerously close.
She thudded down to the ground in front
of Prince Paulsgrave
and hop-walked towards him
until he was pressed up
against the black rock of the cave.

"You dare to come here
after all this time.
You dare to face me
after what you did."

"It's not his fault!"
said Queen Araminta,
running to her frog prince's side.
"It's not his fault
that you love him
but he never loved you.
You cannot keep cursing my family
because of your unrequited love."

"LOVE!!!!"

shouted Aunty,
and the cave shook
as her caw became a callous laugh
devoid of all humour.

"LOVE had nothing to do with it.
I never loved your bug-eyed prince.
My only interest in him
was what he stole from me.
He stole from me
my Eye of Grimm."

The frog prince Paulsgrave started
to gurgle deep in his throat
as he dragged his bloated belly backwards,
heading for the cave's exit.

´Is this true?´
asked Queen Araminta,
turning on her prince.

"Of course it's true,"
screeched Aunty.
"Look at him."

Eshe looked from Aunty
to the frog prince
and back again
and a story started to unfold.
She had never known how Aunty
became a harpy,
but she knew that a sorceress
separated from her Eye of Grimm
was always at risk of being transformed,
as were those who didn't know how
to use an Eye of Grimm with care.

"Aunty never transformed you.
You tried to use the Eye of Grimm
but had no idea what you were doing.
You transformed yourself!"

Something looking like rage
rolled up into Prince Paulsgrave's horrid face.

"Of course I took it.
We're supposed to live in the shadow
of you forest people,
you spell-tricksters,
you word-wielders.
We're supposed to trust you
and your magic,
supposed to trust you'll never use it against us."

Queen Araminta
seemed to get taller
as anger and frustration filled her.

"Everything we've been through,
every injustice our family has endured...
My home turned to splinters,
our daughter growing up without a father,
the years I prayed for you,
came to you,
hoping to save you,

never knowing
that it was all because of you.
The whispers I endured
from my own kingdom —
the gossip, the rumours,
all because you're no more
than a common thief."

A ragged splinter of purple light
tore through the air
from Aunty's wingtips
to Prince Paulsgrave,
lifting him up into the air.

"For years I've suffered,
but now I will have my revenge."

"Please stop!" begged Queen Araminta.

But Eshe could see it was no good.
The deep magic that Aunty had used
over the years
had warped not just her body
but also, her MIND!

"I believe you have something of mine,"
said Aunty,
a cruel, solid look
settling into her eyes.
A spiky ball of purple
luminescence was building and crackling
threateningly as she pulsed her wings.

"Please, Aunty, don't!" yelled Eshe.

153

A sound like something between
a roar and a screech issued forth from
Aunty's beak,
as she closed her eyes
and seemed to be battling
against something inside her.

"He must pay!"
she shrieked.

> "And he has.
> But don't become the thing
> he always feared you were."

The spiky purple ball started to fade
as Aunty closed her eyes and began to mutter
words of magic.

Prince Paulsgrave began to glow from within.
A bright yellow light

pulsed in his stomach
and travelled slowly
up to his froggy chest
and then his froggy throat
until he suddenly belched
and a large golden ball
came shooting out of his mouth.

"You tried to use my Eye of Grimm
but you had no idea of its power.
You swallowed it,
thinking it would make you all-powerful,
but it changed you
in the same way
that being apart from it
changed me."
said Aunty.

The golden ball sped to Aunty
and hovered above her
as she wound a spell
within its glow.

"Take me, Eye,
as you see me,
all feathers and talons and beak.
Lift me high
and renew me,
remove the caws from my speech.
See me new,
make me whole,
put hands where feathers now ruffle.
Remove the bird
that covers me,
turn my claws to feet that can shuffle."

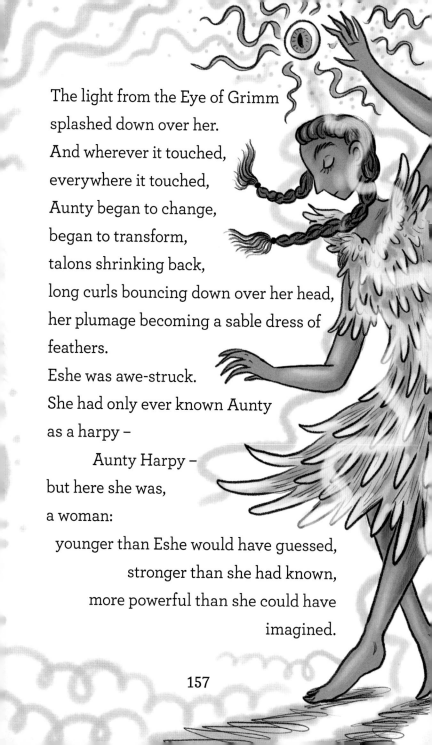

The light from the Eye of Grimm
splashed down over her.
And wherever it touched,
everywhere it touched,
Aunty began to change,
began to transform,
talons shrinking back,
long curls bouncing down over her head,
her plumage becoming a sable dress of
feathers.
Eshe was awe-struck.
She had only ever known Aunty
as a harpy –
    Aunty Harpy –
but here she was,
a woman:
    younger than Eshe would have guessed,
        stronger than she had known,
        more powerful than she could have
            imagined.

She looked powerful
in her dress of harpy feathers.
The Eye of Grimm
floated down and rested in her palm.

She gazed at it
like an old friend returned,
like the kiss of a long-lost soulmate.

The frog prince Paulsgrave
was in a spluttering heap on the floor,
coughing and hacking.

"It's out of me at last.
So why haven't I changed back?"

"Because you lack knowledge.
You misused the eye for your own ends
and you paid the price."

Aunty glared at him with daggers in her eyes.

"Having my Eye of Grimm
taken from me
made me a monster,
warped my mind,
put a beak on my mouth
and a curse on my being,
made me do horrendous things."

Aunty turned to Queen Araminta.

"I am sorry for the tragedy
that has befallen
your family."

Z Z Z Z

"I am sorry, too," said the queen.
"But it is clear now that it was
our own doing."

"Enough of this,"
croaked the prince.
"You have your ball now,
so change me back.
I beg you. Please."

The frog prince Paulsgrave clasped his flabby
green hands together as he pleaded.

And then a rumble was heard from outside.
A rumble that sounded like a moan,
like a moan made up of many sounds,
a deep sonorous moan...
No, not a moan –
a snore
made up of a million voices.

CHAPTER 14

Return of the Twelve

Eshe
was first outside the cave
and choked with shock.
The whole of Skyblade mountain
was surrounded
by a sea of green
punctuated by red –
deep, blood-red roses
floating above
a thicket of thorns
as far as the eye could see.

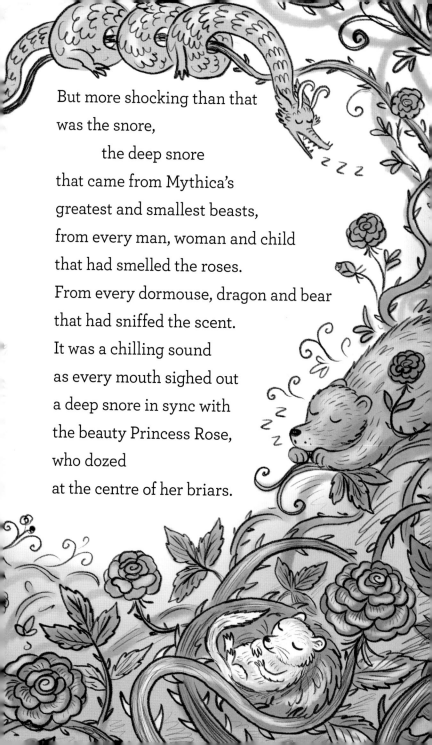

But more shocking than that
was the snore,
        the deep snore
that came from Mythica's
greatest and smallest beasts,
from every man, woman and child
that had smelled the roses.
From every dormouse, dragon and bear
that had sniffed the scent.
It was a chilling sound
as every mouth sighed out
a deep snore in sync with
the beauty Princess Rose,
who dozed
at the centre of her briars.

Aunty and Queen Araminta joined
Eshe outside.

"Nothing I've done to try
and stop this has worked.
My vision has come true
exactly as I saw it."

"You are too hard on yourself.
You did what you felt was right.
We all had our parts to play
and now there is nothing we can do.
It's become too big
and we are not strong enough.
Soon we, too, will be lost to the nightmare."

A panting was heard from below,
a panting and a sighing
different from the terrifying
rumble of slumber

that beat out a dirge across the whole of
Mythica.

Eshe watched as, from below,
came first one,
then two,
then three,
then four,
then all twelve of her sisters …

huffing and puffing
up Skyblade mountain.

"This mountain is so steep,"
complained sister number three
called Three-eena, who was blessed
with a third eye at the centre of her forehead.

"Ain't that the truth,"
said sister number twelve called
Twelve-olet, who always carried a personal
buffet.

"Sisters, you are here! You're OK,"
called Eshe, desperate to hug them all
but all too aware of the years
that had passed without so much
as a word from them.
The sisters stopped when they saw her
and an awkward silence yawned
between them ...
until sister number five,
called Fivanna, who was forever chewing
something, said,
"Eshe, sister, we've been looking for you.
We were so wrong. We should have listened;
we should have believed you."

Her other sisters crowded in
and smiled and hugged her,
whispering their apologies
and holding her tight,

                          tight,

                                tight.

"This is all lovely,"
said Queen Araminta.
"But my daughter's vines are creeping upon us
and very soon we, too, shall fall
into the eternal slumber."

"Maybe not,"
said Aunty,
as she stood
head and shoulders
above the rest,
her Eye of Grimm
shining in her hand.

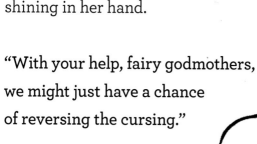

"With your help, fairy godmothers,
we might just have a chance
of reversing the cursing."

The mass of snores
rising up from Mythica

was becoming a chilling heartbeat,
a dark drum roll
of nightmare and fear.

Eshe and her sisters stood beside
Aunty and all of them took out
their Eyes of Grimm.
The fourteen balls glistened and shone
as the thorns of Creeping Beauty
inched their way up Mount Skyblade.

Eshe didn't stop to think,
didn't hesitate.
She began to freestyle a spell
and as she did so,
all the Eyes of Grimm
started to take on an intensity in their glow,
becoming bright,
brighter than bright,
brighter than fireworks in broad daylight!

Something like a clap of thunderous thunder
echoed through her,
through her sisters,
through Aunty
and all of them were zapped ...

into a nightmare.

CHAPTER 15

A Thorny Nightmare

Eshe opened her eyes to find
herself alone!
In a maze,
    an amazing maze,
        an amazing maze of vicious thorns.
The sky above was dark and thundersome
and the ground below
was twig-filled and thornysome.

Eshe felt fear streak through her.
She ran down one winding,
prickly avenue and then another,
calling out loudly the whole time,
calling out for her sisters.
She turned left, then right,
all the time the thorns
closing in until
she found herself
in a circular clearing
edged in prickles.

"Here you all are,"
she breathed, as she saw her sisters
standing around the edges, silent,
their heads down.
But as they lifted them,
she saw that their eyes
were as dark green
as the leaves of roses.

When Queen Araminta opened her eyes,
she found herself in her castle
the way it used to be,
made of stone and rock,
a fire burning in the hearth
and a chill wind blowing through the rooms.
Rose! she thought
and ran from room to room
calling out for her daughter,
hoping to find her.
But there was nothing;
there was no one –
just a humming,
buzzing sound from the walls,
from the bricks,
from the cracks between the bricks
where vines were worming their way out.
On their tips
were blood-red buds
that bloomed into roses.

As the queen gazed at them,
the hum and buzz got louder,
becoming speech.
And as the roses opened and closed their petals,
like red-lipped mouths, they started to speak!
Started to whisper rumours…

"The queen has made a pact with a devil."

"The queen goes to the forest to dance with demons."

*"The queen is no queen of ours – she's more concerned
about her daughter."*

"What happened to her husband?"

"He ran off!"

"She's evil!"

"She's a witch."

The queen got on her knees, blocked her
ears and screamed.

179

When Aunty opened her eyes,
she found herself back in her old home
in the woods.
She was looking in a mirror
admiring her human skin,
appreciating her human face –
a face she hadn't seen in so long,
a face she had missed.

But as she looked,
she noticed vines
creeping around the mirror's edge –
thick, sappy vines
with sharp pointed tips.

Her reflection started to change.
Her lips started to purse,
started to harden,
started to beakify.
Feathers started erupting all around her face ...

until she was once again
a harpy.

Aunty stared at her reflection
and roared as tears fell
down her feathered face.

Eshe's sisters were in fact not with Eshe.
They were each experiencing their own
magical nightmares...

Oneie was searching
for her dog, who was missing.

Tutu's tattoos
started slithering and hissing.

Three-eena's third eye
felt terribly sore.

Forula's colourful bows
all fell to the floor.

Fivanna's earrings
lost their sparkle and shine.

Josix's card tricks
didn't work all the time.

Sevoona's sweet voice
grew terribly dull.

Eightina's ring fingers
wouldn't fit in her ring holes!

Jas-nine's pet llama
started to spit!

Tentoria was annoyed
and had a tantrum fit!

Elevenora's lovely smile
became a monstrous frown.

Twelve-olet's buffet
got turned upside down.

And all the while,
Eshe was trapped in her nightmare
with twelve nightmarish versions of her sisters,
all with deep-green eyes
totally unlike her sisters' hazel-brown eyes,
all shouting at her that she was unlucky,
going beyond their usual teasing,
devoid of any of the love she knew
they had for her.

You brought shame on the family.

*We'd all be better off
without unlucky sister thirteen.*

*Why don't you stay in the woods
alone, for ever?*

Their words hurt.
Cut her deep.

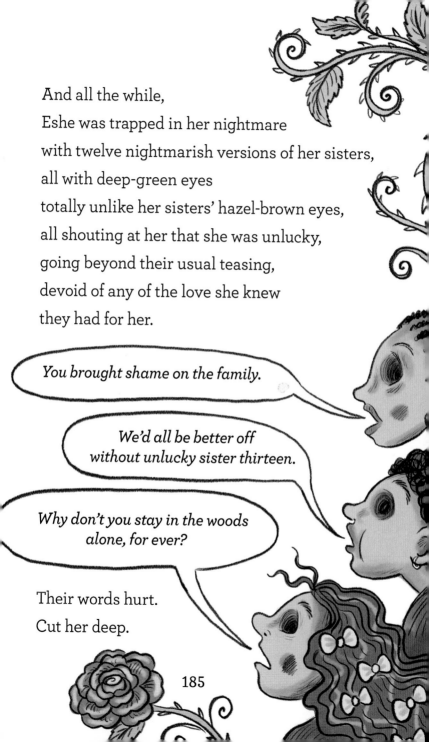

185

They spoke to her of the years
she had spent alone in the woods,
making herself believe
that her exile was for the best,
that her sisters were better off
without her.

But in her chest
she felt a heat
which became a glow.
And from her heart,
her Eye of Grimm
materialized.
In this nightmare world,
where everything was
dark and sombre,
her Eye of Grimm
shone and glowed.
And as it glowed, she found
herself getting braver,

felt herself standing taller.
She turned to her nightmare sisters and
yelled,

"I'm not unlucky.
I'm strong and I'm powerful
and I belong."

And just like that,
her fake sisters
started to wither
and crisp like dried leaves,
and their bodies drifted away
like smoke on the wind.

And that's when Eshe heard a sobbing.

CHAPTER 16

Protectors of Mythica

An opening appeared
in the thorns
and the sobbing that Eshe could hear
got louder.

Eshe ran through
and found herself
in a bedroom,
a grand bedroom,
a grand, blood-red bedroom
with a cloying sickly-sweet scent.

Princess Rose's bed
was itself a giant rose,
the sheets made up of huge soft petals.
And sitting on top of it,
in deluges of tears,
was Princess Rose.

Eshe approached
and straight away noticed
how the floor was thorned
and woody and sharp.
The thorns crunched and snapped
under her steps
like brittle glass.

Princess Rose was hunched over on the bed,
her hair covering her face,
her hands cupping her bare feet.
Eshe went to her
and sat gingerly on the edge of the bed.

"Princess Rose? Are you OK?"

Her sobs came in deep,
heartfelt thrums.

"I can't find my slippers,"
she managed between sobs.
"And the floor is so sharp.
And I've been here for so long."

Eshe peeled Princess Rose's hands from
her feet and saw that her soles were bloody
with thorn pricks.

"Your feet!"
she gasped.
"We have to get you out of here."

All the while
in the other nightmares:

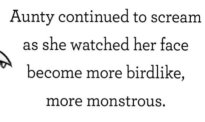

Queen Araminta
was still being plagued
by eerie, whispered rumours.

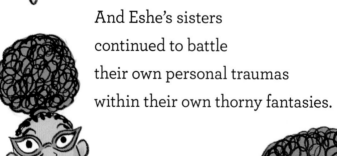

Aunty continued to scream
as she watched her face
become more birdlike,
more monstrous.

And Eshe's sisters
continued to battle
their own personal traumas
within their own thorny fantasies.

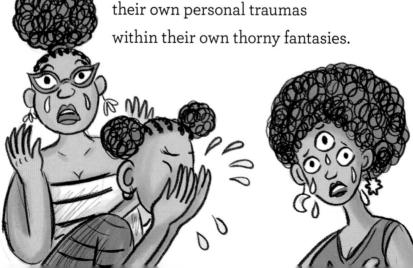

Eshe was the only one
who had faced her terrors,
the only one who could break them all free.
So, she held up her Eye of Grimm,
stared deep into its golden light,
and felt the warmth and love within:
of family,
of her mother and father,
of her sisters,
of her ancestors,
of all who came before her.
She could feel her sisters now
trapped in their nightmares
but still with love in their hearts for her.
She could feel Aunty's strength
and Queen Araminta's own royal power,
all striving, all wanting this nightmare to end.
It was power that she could feel.
And she could use it.

Eshe let that love and strength and power
reach its way through her,
let it tingle in her fingertips
and began to freestyle a spell...

"Thorns, begone,
all brambles and prickles.
Roses wither,
all flowers and petals.
Vines diminish,
all creep and tackle.
End this war,
this slumber battle."

There was an almighty thunderous roar
like something snapping,
giving way,
making room,
breaking.
The first thing Eshe noticed
was a smile blooming onto Princess Rose's face
as all the thorns on the floor popped,
as bright yellow flower buds
pushed their way up and out of them.
And a new scent started to fill the chamber –
a warm, refreshing scent,
of lemon and verbena,
of lime and summer
that made Eshe's eyes feel heavy
as she fell asleep in the nightmare ...

and so woke up in the real world
wide awake.

She was back
on the mountainside
with Aunty and Queen Araminta
and her sisters
all blinking and rubbing their eyes
as the combined glow
from their Eyes of Grimm
started to diminish.

A strange rustling sound could be heard
as the thorny vines
that surrounded Mount Skyblade
started to shrink back,
to wither and die.
Eshe used her telescope
and in the distance spied
Princess Rose sinking down,
her eyes open
as her vines gathered back into her,
becoming legs and arms.

"You did it! You saved us," said Queen Araminta, grabbing Eshe by both hands.

"No, we did it! It took us all.
You, My Queen … Aunty … my sisters …
it would have been impossible without you all.
Without your power,
the power of love and friendship,
family and strength."

As they stood listening
to the last snore
die away from the land,
a throaty shuffling
came scrambling behind them.
It was the frog prince Paulsgrave.

"You did it! You saved us.
Now you can save me, oh powerful
and wise godmothers.

198

Change me back, please."

Eshe, Aunty,
Queen Araminta and
Eshe's twelve sisters eyed
Paulsgrave with a mixture of disgust and pity.

"There is nothing we can do for you,"
said Eshe.
"You swallowed an Eye of Grimm
that wasn't yours
and it changed you,
revealed your true nature.
In time, with good behaviour,
the effects may fade.
But it will take hard work
and a pure heart
and you can start
by returning your queen home
and seeing that your daughter is OK."

"We will go straight away,"
said Queen Araminta.
"I cannot thank you enough.
What you have done today
will have repercussions
across the whole kingdom."

Eshe never suspected
Paulsgrave's slimy tongue
which shot out lightning fast,
aiming straight for her Eye of Grimm.
But it was the queen
who intervened this time,
her royal hand catching his tongue quick
and wrapping it tight around her fist.

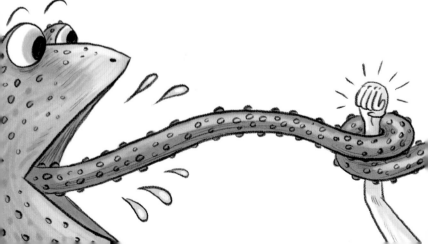

"You have much to learn,
my prince.
Learning that you will do
in the dungeons
until you have proven your heart
can be made pure."

Using his tongue as a rein,
Queen Araminta mounted
the frog prince
as he gurgled his apologies,
and leapt off towards her castle,
her daughter and home.

Eshe was left on the mountainside
with Aunty and her sisters,
one of fourteen fairy godmothers
each with an Eye of Grimm,
each determined
to protect all of Mythica with their powers
and to never again
let nightmares rule.

Eshe watched as the queen bounded away,
watched as the vines shrank back,
pleased to know that her actions
hadn't been in vain,
that she had once again saved the world.
But this time,
things were different...

Her sisters hugged her close.

"All this time your predictions have been true?"
they squealed with glee.

"Absolutely," said Aunty.
"She is a very gifted seer and has saved the
world more times than you can imagine."

"Well, you must tell us all about it,"
said her sisters
as they hugged her tight, tight, tight,
tighter than they had ever hugged her before.
And now fourteen fairy godmothers
made their way home,
smiling with the knowledge
that together they were unstoppable,
together they'd be able to uproot any misdeed,
together they could protect the whole of
Mythica, helping the kingdom grow
and bloom.

EPILOGUE

Back so soon?!
Hope you're not too disturbed
by that sprouting tale
of brave fairy godmothers
and a monstrous prince.
I hope the tale
made its prickly point!
That no bad deed
goes UNPRUN-ISHED!!!

MWAHAHAHAHAHAHA!!!

May your actions need no pruning,
my rotted readers.

I must leave you now.
I can hear my tales reaching
deeper into the library –

more unloved books
are changing,
rusting, deteriorating
and yet becoming
something frightful,
something wonderfully gory ...
and new.

I look forward
to seeing you
next time for some more ...

Fairy Tales Gone Bad!